Dirty Bertie

MASCOT!

For Bertie, for all the years of fun and laughs
~ D R and A M

STRIPES PUBLISHING
An imprint of the Little Tiger Group
1 Coda Studios, 189 Munster Road,
London SW6 6AW

A paperback original
First published in Great Britain in 2018

Characters created by David Roberts
Text copyright © Alan MacDonald, 2018
Illustrations copyright © David Roberts, 2018

ISBN: 978-1-84715-811-6

Printed and bound in the UK.

10 9 8 7 6 5 4 3 2 1

Dirty Bertie

MASCOT!

DAVID ROBERTS WRITTEN BY ALAN MACDONALD

Collect all the Dirty Bertie books!

Contents

MASCOT!

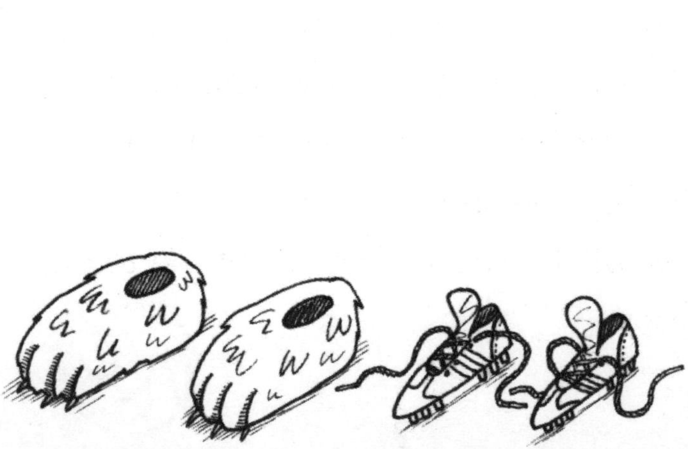

CHAPTER 1

Mum came into the kitchen carrying the post.

"Oh, Bertie, you've got a letter," she said.

Bertie hardly ever got any post apart from at birthdays and Christmas. He tore open the envelope.

"Wow!" he cried. "They want me to be a mascot!"

"That's nice," said Mum. "You've got jam on your face."

"A mascot for the school team?" asked Dad.

"No, for Rovers," replied Bertie. He read out the letter…

You're invited to be Rovers' match day mascot for the game against Mudchester City…

"Who's Rovers?" yawned Suzy.

"Pudsley Rovers!" said Dad. "Our local team – they're in Division One!"

"But why choose Bertie as their mascot?" asked Mum.

Bertie didn't have a clue. Then he remembered – months ago he'd put his name down for something to do with football. Darren had done it, too – he'd been wildly excited about the chance of being picked.

"I think I entered a competition," said Bertie. "Anyway, what's a mascot?"

"It's a huge honour," explained Dad. "Every team has a lucky mascot. You run out with the players and line up before kick-off."

This didn't sound that exciting to
Bertie. He had to line up before school
every day.

"Do I kick the ball?" he asked.

"No! You're not *playing*!" said Dad.

"Do I blow the whistle then?"

"That's the referee's job," said Dad.

"Well, *what do I do*?" Bertie wanted
to know.

"I've told you, you cheer your team
on and bring them luck," said Dad.
"You'll probably meet Larry Lion."

"There's a *LION*?" said Bertie.

That would certainly make the game
more exciting. The players would have
to run for their lives!

"It's not a *real* lion," said Dad. "Rovers'
team mascot is Larry Lion. It's a man
dressed up in a lion costume."

Bertie frowned. "But I thought *I* was the mascot?"

"You're the *junior match day mascot*, which is different each time," Dad explained. "Larry Lion is the *team mascot* – he's there for every game."

Bertie thought it all sounded a bit complicated.

"Why can't I be the lion?" he asked.

"Sorry, I don't think that's what they want," said Dad.

"They might," said Bertie. "The letter doesn't say I *can't* be the lion. Anyway, they haven't heard me roar yet. ROARRRRR!"

Mum and Dad covered their ears. They hoped Bertie wasn't going to get too carried away.

CHAPTER 2

Bertie couldn't wait to tell his friends on Monday morning.

"Guess what," he said, on the way to school. "I'm going to be a mascot!"

"You?" said Eugene. "What for?"

"For Rovers," answered Bertie. "Dad says they're really famous."

"I know who they are," said Darren.

Dirty Bertie

"My dad takes me to all the home games. But who says you're the mascot?"

"I got a letter on Saturday," said Bertie. "It must have been that competition we entered."

Darren's mouth fell open. "That's so unfair! You only entered because I did. You don't know anything about football!"

"I *do*! I played for the school team," argued Bertie.

"Only once, because no one else would go in goal," said Darren.

"Anyway, they picked me," said Bertie. "I've got to lead the teams out for the kick-up."

"The kick-*off*," said Darren.

"But that's not the best bit," Bertie beamed. "I'm going to dress up as a lion!"

"What?" said Eugene.

"You don't mean Larry Lion?" gasped Darren. "They want you to be *Larry Lion*?"

"That's right," said Bertie. "There are two mascots but I'm definitely going to be the lion one."

Darren and Eugene could hardly believe it. Not only was Bertie going to be a mascot – he got to wear a lion costume.

"Larry Lion is a legend," said Darren. "He gets the crowd laughing and cheering. He can even juggle a football!"

Bertie hoped they didn't want him to juggle. But he was good at making his friends laugh so he'd just have to stick to that.

"Well, I'll be there on Saturday," said Darren.

"Me too," said Eugene. "Just think, thousands of people will be watching you."

"Thousands?" said Bertie.

He had no idea. When the school team played, only two parents came to watch. Being Rovers' mascot was even better than he'd thought – he'd be

Dirty Bertie

famous! People would stop him in the street to ask for his autograph. He might even wear his lion costume to school for a few weeks.

CHAPTER 3

The week before the big game passed
slowly. Bertie drove his family mad with
what he called his "lion practice". He
woke his parents early in the morning
with his roaring. He made Suzy scream
by jumping out from behind the
bathroom door. At mealtimes he even
took to eating like a lion.

Dirty Bertie

"Bertie, use your knife and fork," sighed Mum.

"I can't," said Bertie. "Lions eat with their paws."

"Not in this house, and don't slobber when you eat."

"Shlurp, shlurp!" said Bertie, licking his plate.

Dad shook his head. "I wish I'd never mentioned Larry Lion," he groaned.

On Saturday Dad drove Bertie to the Rovers stadium.

"Just do what they tell you and try not to get overexcited," he warned.

Bertie didn't see how it was possible to be *overexcited*. After all, he was going to be a lion!

Dirty Bertie

At the ground they were shown into the manager's office. Barry Ball was a big bulldog of a man with a firm handshake.

"So, Bertie, you like football, do you?" he asked.

"Yes," replied Bertie. "And I'm pretty good at roaring."

"Roaring?" said the manager, looking confused.

Dirty Bertie

"He's been excited all week about dressing up as Larry Lion," Dad explained.

"I'm sure that won't be necessary," laughed Barry Ball. "Let's go downstairs and you can meet the lads."

In the dressing room Bertie was introduced to the Rovers' players. To him they all looked like giants. The captain was called Kyle.

"Bertie, put it there!" said Kyle, giving him a high five. "Let's find you a Rovers kit, shall we?"

Dirty Bertie

Bertie changed into the Rovers yellow shirt and shorts. It looked good but he was keen to see the rest of his costume.

"What about my lion's head?" he asked.

Barry Ball smiled. "That's what I was saying, you don't have to wear a costume," he said. "Anyway, it's far too big."

"It's okay, I'd *like* to wear it," said Bertie.

"Yes, but that's Tommy's job. He's Larry Lion but he's off with a bad back this week," explained the manager. "Anyway, you look fine in football kit."

Bertie's shoulders drooped. After all his practice, they didn't want him to be the lion. It was so unfair. He'd set his heart on wearing the costume and

Dirty Bertie

a boring football kit wasn't the same.
Worst of all, his friends would think he'd
made the whole thing up.

Dirty Bertie

"I'd better get to my seat," said Dad. "Try to stay out of trouble, Bertie, and I'll see you at half-time."

Bertie sat kicking his legs while the players got changed. He wondered where they kept the lion costume. It must be somewhere if Tommy wasn't wearing it. He peeped into the next room and noticed a row of grey lockers. Maybe he'd just take a little look around…

The first three lockers were empty but in the next he struck gold. A lion costume hung on a hook, complete with a gigantic head. Surely there was no harm in just trying it on? Quickly, he slipped into the suit and pulled on the head. He could just see out through a gap in the mouth.

"Hey, Bertie, where are you?" called Barry Ball. "We're ready to go!"

Uh oh, they were calling him. Bertie looked at his huge furry feet and paws. There wasn't time to take off the costume, he'd just have to go as he was. He plodded back into the dressing room.

25

When the players saw him they all burst out laughing.

"I told you, it's way too big for you!" said Barry Ball.

"Oh, let him wear it, boss," grinned Kyle. "Who's going to know it's not Tommy?"

He took Bertie's paw and led him out. Bertie heard the clatter of football studs as they went down a long tunnel. Ahead he could see bright lights and hear music playing. They stepped out into the vast stadium. This was it…

CHAPTER 4

A great roar from the crowd greeted the teams. Bertie glowed with pride and waved a paw. The players ran off to warm up, kicking a ball to each other. Bertie stood waving to everyone. He hoped that Darren and Eugene could see him.

THUMP! A football landed at his feet.

Dirty Bertie

"Go on. Take a shot, Bertie," said
Kyle.

Bertie wasn't brilliant at shooting and
he was wearing giant furry feet. Still,
thousands of people were watching.
He ran at the ball and hoofed it with
all his might. It missed the goal but hit
someone on the back. The "someone"
turned round and glared at him – it was
the referee.

Dirty Bertie

"Oops, sorry!" cried Bertie. He danced away swishing his tail.

Bertie joined the teams as they lined up. He shook the City players' hands and they shook him by the paw. Then the referee blew his whistle to start the game and Bertie's starring role was over.

He stood on the sidelines watching the ball zip back and forth. It was hard to see much from inside the lion's head. After about twenty minutes, he heard a big cheer. Bertie looked round and saw the ball in the back of the net. GOAL! He jumped up and down and did his lion dance. But hang on a minute – the Rovers players were all holding their heads in their hands. The ball was in *their* goal – it was City who'd scored!

A hand tapped him on the shoulder.

It was the linesman with his yellow flag.

"I can't see the game with your big head in the way," he grumbled.

"But I'm the mascot!" said Bertie.

"I don't care who you are, stand over there behind the goal."

Bertie trailed off. He didn't see why he couldn't stand wherever he wanted.

"BERTIE! HEY, BERTIE!"

Bertie turned round. Darren and Eugene were calling and waving from the crowd. Bertie waved back. Then he did his lion dance, waggling his bottom and making his tail swing round and round.

"HEY!" shouted the linesman. "For the last time, keep away from the pitch!"

Bertie sighed. There was no pleasing some people.

At half-time, Dad arrived to check
how he was getting on. The referee
came over and gave Bertie a lecture
about not standing near the touchline.

"Sorry. He's never been a mascot before," Dad explained. "He just gets a bit overexcited."

The second half began. Bertie stood behind the City goal, trying to keep out of the way. The game seemed to be going nowhere. The crowd had gone quiet and Rovers were heading for a 1-0 defeat. As the mascot Bertie felt he ought to help. Perhaps if he danced or did a cartwheel the crowd would make more noise? He tried a cartwheel but it was more of a bad head over heels. He tried it again then spun round waving his tail. When he stopped, he found he'd made himself dizzy. He staggered a few steps to one side.

"HEY! GET OFF THE PITCH, YOU IDIOT!"

Dirty Bertie

The linesman was shouting again. Bertie swung round…

THUD!

Something thumped him hard on the side of the head.

A split second later there was a deafening roar. Bertie sat up. The ball was in the net and the City goalkeeper was face down on the grass. For a moment Bertie couldn't think what had happened. Then a scrum of Rovers players were jumping on top of him.

"Great goal, Bertie!" said Kyle.

Bertie realized he'd wandered on
to the pitch. The ball must have hit his
head and bounced into the goal. He'd
scored for Rovers!

The goal caused an almighty row. The
City players crowded round the referee
arguing and pointing. The referee went
over to the linesman. Finally, he gave

the goal because he couldn't think of anything in the rules about lions.

Bertie's moment of glory didn't last long however. The referee sent him off to a chorus of boos. Bertie waved one last time as he trudged off. It wasn't *his* fault the ball had hit him. He'd never even seen it!

Ten minutes later the whistle went and the game ended in a draw. The Rovers fans cheered while the City fans booed the referee loudly.

Bertie stood by the tunnel as the Rovers players came off. They all shook his hand or clapped him on the back.

"Nice header, Bertie! We should sign you up!" said Kyle.

Bertie took off his lion's head and costume. His face was hot but he was grinning.

Dad arrived looking flustered.

"Can I be mascot again next week?" Bertie asked.

"I think maybe once was enough," said Dad.

"Anyway, Tommy will be wanting his job back," added Barry Ball.

The referee was still red-faced and arguing with the City players. When he caught sight of Bertie he pushed past them.

"Uh oh, I think he's coming over," said Dad. "Time we were going, Bertie. Come on!"

They left the ground and hurried to the car park.

Dirty Bertie

Bertie looked down. In the race to get away he'd forgotten to remove his giant furry lion's feet.

"Oh well," he said. "You never know when I might need them."

CHAPTER 1

Bertie strolled home, swinging his bag.
At last, the summer holidays! he thought.
Six whole weeks without lessons,
homework or Miss Boot telling him to
stop talking. Stuffed in his bag was a
leaflet that she'd handed out at home
time. Bertie hadn't bothered paying
much attention – letters from school

were usually boring.

Back home he settled down in front of the TV. Mum came in.

"What's this?" she asked, waving the leaflet. "I found it in your bag."

"Oh yes, Miss Boot gave it to us," said Bertie. "It's a camp or something – I wasn't really listening."

BRIGHT SPARKS CAMP

Make friends and have fun learning with other bright sparks!

Dirty Bertie

Mum read it through. Bertie had never been on a summer camp and this one sounded educational. He certainly needed to do something about his school marks. His last report said: "Bertie's work has actually gone *backwards* this year."

"This sounds fun, Bertie," she said. "Would you like to go?"

"ME?" said Bertie.

"Yes, it'll give you something to do in the holidays," said Mum.

Dirty Bertie

Bertie thought he had plenty to do already. For starters, there were a million TV shows he wanted to watch.

"I'll be busy," he said.

"It's only for a week," said Mum. "I expect there'll be lots of games and activities. You might even learn something."

Bertie frowned. He wouldn't mind learning how to jet ski but that seemed unlikely.

"No thanks, I'd rather stay at home," he said.

"But you might enjoy it," Mum persisted. "Don't you want to make some new friends?"

"I like my *old* friends," replied Bertie. "Anyway, when we went camping it rained all the time and the toilets stunk."

"Summer camp's not like that," said Mum. "I expect you sleep in rooms with comfy beds."

"I like sleeping in my *own* bed," said Bertie.

He didn't see why Mum was so keen for him to go to summer camp. Anyone would think she wanted to get rid of him!

Dad came in.

"Take a look at this," said Mum. "I thought Bertie might like to go."

"I wouldn't!" said Bertie.

"It sounds great," said Dad. "I wish I'd had the chance to go to summer camp."

"But I'd rather stay here with my friends," argued Bertie.

"Well maybe Darren or Eugene would like to go?" suggested Mum. "I could speak to their parents."

Bertie sighed. He wished Miss Boot had never given out the leaflets!

Later that evening Mum found Bertie in his room.

"Darren can't go but Eugene's parents love the idea," she reported. "So it's all agreed, you two are off to camp."

Bertie sighed. He didn't seem to have much choice in the matter.

CHAPTER 2

At the weekend Bertie discussed the camp with his friends.

"It's not fair!" grumbled Darren, "I never get to go anywhere!"

"You're lucky, I didn't ask to go," said Bertie. "My parents practically made me."

"At least we'll both be there," said

Eugene. "Maybe they've got a swimming pool."

"My cousin says summer camp is fantastic," said Darren. "He did rock climbing and zip wiring. Every night they cooked over a campfire."

"Really?" said Bertie. The leaflet hadn't said anything about zip wires or rock climbing.

"You'll have a great time while I'm stuck at home," grumbled Darren.

"My parents keep saying I might learn something," said Bertie. "What does that mean?"

On the first Monday of the holidays, Bertie and Eugene waited for the coach to arrive. Bertie had never been away

Dirty Bertie

from his family before. He couldn't
imagine how they'd cope without him.
He stared at the other campers, waiting
with their parents. They all looked smart
and well behaved. Strangely, a number
of them were clutching pencil cases.

"Who are all these kids?"
whispered Bertie.

Eugene shrugged. "They must be
from other schools," he said. "It
doesn't look like anyone else
from our school's going."

At last the coach arrived. The man in charge was called Mr Twig, who made them line up.

"Be good, Bertie," said Dad.

"I'm sure you'll have a wonderful time," said Mum, hugging him.

"Try not to work too hard," grinned Suzy.

Bertie frowned. This was a holiday – he wasn't planning to do any work!

On the coach he settled into a seat next to Eugene. At the last minute a boy climbed on, looking out of breath. Bertie glanced up.

"OH NO! Not Know-All Nick!" he groaned.

Nick was the last person he wanted at camp. He ducked down in his seat but it was too late.

"Oh hello, Bertie!" Nick sneered. "Don't tell me *you're* coming to camp?"

"I was, until *you* arrived," replied Bertie.

"I go to Bright Sparks every summer," boasted Nick. "In fact it was me who told Miss Boot about it. Mum says it's good for me to mix with other clever children."

Bertie rolled his eyes.

"I thought you'd hate summer camp," said Eugene. "You don't even like games or sports."

"Sports?" Nick sniggered. "Oh no, I think you've got the wrong idea. It's not *that* sort of summer camp."

"Then what sort is it?" asked Bertie.

"Bright Sparks is a summer school for clever children," said Nick. "We do maths, science, spelling – all my favourite things in fact. I'm sure *you're* going to love it, Bertie!"

A *summer school* – with children like Nick? Bertie felt a wave of panic. He looked around wildly but the coach was moving off. Suddenly it all made sense. No wonder Miss Boot was keen to hand out the leaflets. No wonder his parents

Dirty Bertie

wanted him to go. He'd been tricked!
Bright Sparks was a school for swots!
He stared at his fellow campers on the
bus, clutching their new pencil cases.
This was all a terrible mistake.

"STOP THE BUS!" he wailed. "I want
to get off!"

CHAPTER 3

The coach turned down a long drive
and came to a stop. Bertie stared at an
ancient school topped with turrets and
towers. It looked older than his gran.

"At least we won't be sleeping in
tents," said Eugene.

"No, but we're back at school!"
moaned Bertie.

Dirty Bertie

Nick poked him in the back. "I hope you're not going to moan all the time," he said. "Bright Sparks always look on the bright side."

Mr Twig took them up to their dormitory. Iron beds sat in two rows in a dark, chilly room. Notices on the walls said:

"Tidy children have tidy minds" and *"Bright sparks always give their best!"*

"Well, this is home for the week," said Mr Twig. "You've got half an hour to make your beds and fold your clothes before assembly."

Bertie had never made a bed in his life. Summer camp was like joining the army!

Downstairs they filed into the grand hall under the eye of the teachers. The campers sat up straight and folded their arms. Miss Cram, the camp director, stood up and beamed.

"Welcome campers, old and new," she said. "Some summer camps are all about idle pleasure — swimming, campfires and zip wires, that kind of thing. Bright Sparks is different. If you enjoy hard work and getting top marks then you've come to the right place."

"Hooray!" cheered Nick.

"Help!" gulped Eugene.

"Get me out of here!" moaned Bertie.

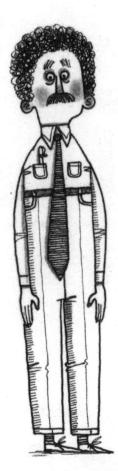

"Now I'm sure you want to see your timetables, so Mr Twig will hand them out," Miss Cram went on.

Bertie was given a timetable with his name on. The day began with "Fun with maths", followed by spelling, grammar, science, more maths (advanced) and a test to round off the day.

"I love tests!" chirped Nick. "It's just like school!"

"No," said Bertie. "It's even worse."

At least at school they got to go home. Here there was no escape from teachers all day and night. Where were the zip wires and campfires Darren had talked about? Nick leaned closer.

"So aren't you glad you came, Bertie?" he smirked.

Bertie ground his teeth.

Dirty Bertie

$+ - \times \div$

At 7 a.m. the next morning he was woken by a loud bell. Bertie opened his eyes and remembered. Oh no, he was stuck at swot camp and a long day of lessons lay ahead of him.

"Couldn't your mum come and fetch us?" he begged Eugene as they got dressed.

"No chance," said Eugene. "I bet they knew all along this was a swot camp."

Bertie trailed from one lesson to the next. Sometimes they took place outdoors but that meant marching round the field, chanting their times tables. With Miss Comma they played spelling games. You moved up a place if you spelled a word correctly and down a place if you got it wrong. Bertie sunk quickly to the bottom.

Dirty Bertie

Know-All Nick passed him in the corridor.

"Having fun, Bertie?" he jeered. "Can you spell 'Dumbo' yet?"

"Can you spell, 'Get Lost'?" Bertie replied.

Back at the dorm, Bertie lay on his bed. "It's torture!" he groaned.

"I know," said Eugene. "And the worst thing is we're meant to be on holiday!"

Bertie sighed. Six more days of lessons, tests and Nick's ugly face at breakfast. There had to be a way out.

"I know," he said. "We could escape!"

"How?" asked Eugene. "We're miles from anywhere!"

This was true enough. Even if they got out of school they'd probably get lost in the woods. Bertie sat up.

"Wait, what if they *sent* us home?" he said.

"Why would they do that?" asked Eugene.

"They might if we broke the rules," said Bertie. "What if we did something so awful that they'd have to get rid of us?"

Eugene looked anxious. He hated getting into trouble. But Bertie's mind was already racing ahead. What crime would be so bad that Miss Cram would be forced to send them home?

CHAPTER 4

Bertie lay awake half the night but nothing came to him until the following day. In the afternoon Mr Twig was taking them for a nature lesson as part of science.

"I want you each to take one of these jars," he said. "Let's see what insects you can collect for us to study. Caterpillars, slugs, ladybirds, beetles – anything you can find."

Bertie couldn't believe his luck. Finally, this was his kind of lesson – he loved any sort of creepy-crawly. And better still, it had given him a brilliant idea.

Bertie grabbed a jar and followed Eugene outside. They found a rock and rolled it over. Underneath dozens of shiny black beetles crawled around.

"Perfect," said Bertie, scooping some into his jar. He checked no one was watching and hid the jar under a bush.

"What are you doing?" asked Eugene. "We're meant to take that back to class."

"No one will notice," said Bertie. "We can pick it up at the end. You want to get sent home, don't you?"

"Well, yes," said Eugene. "But how are beetles going to help?"

"I'll explain later," said Bertie. "Come on, let's fill your jar so we've got something to show."

That evening Bertie crawled into bed. He glanced across at Eugene and gave him a thumbs up. Eugene slid down under the covers. He could hardly bear to watch.

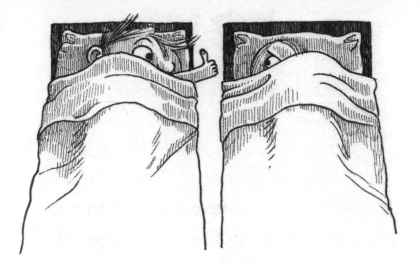

"Lights out, children, no talking," said
Mr Twig. The room was plunged into
darkness. Bertie waited. It shouldn't be
too long now. Three, two, one…

"YEEEARGHHH!" a boy screamed.
"There's something in my bed!"

"HEEELP!" yelled another. "It's
crawling up my leg!"

The lights went back on. All over the
dorm, boys were leaping out of bed and
hopping around as if their pyjamas were
on fire.

Mr Twig saw something black scuttle across the floor and trapped it in his hand.

"Hmm. A ground beetle," he said. "I wonder how that got in?"

He looked around. Only two boys had remained in their beds. One was hiding under the covers while the other seemed to be enjoying the chaos.

"Bertie," said Mr Twig. "Come here. You too, Eugene."

Bertie got out of bed. "Now we're in big trouble!" he grinned.

Early next morning Bertie and Eugene waited outside Miss Cram's office.

"Don't look so worried," whispered Bertie. "She'll probably tell us off, then send us home."

Miss Cram opened the door and beckoned them in.

"Ah, our two practical jokers," she said, taking a seat at her desk. "Mr Twig told

me about your little prank. I suppose
you think putting beetles in someone's
bed is funny?"

"Quite funny," said Bertie.

Miss Cram glared. "We do not tolerate
troublemakers at this camp," she said. "I
am very tempted to send you home."

Whoopee! thought Bertie. *Goodbye
swot camp!*

"However I don't believe in giving up
on children," Miss Cram went on. "So I've
decided to move you to another dorm."

Bertie gaped.

"M-move us?" he stammered.

"That's what I said. I've asked one of
our trusted campers to keep a close eye
on you," said Miss Cram. "He'll be with
you every minute of the day to make
sure you behave."

Dirty Bertie

There was a knock on the door. Bertie looked round. His face fell.

"Hello, Bertie!" smirked Know-All Nick. "We're going to have so much fun together!"

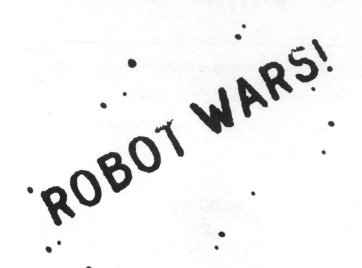

ROBOT WARS!

BOOTOSAURUS

Weight:	15kg
Dimensions:	27cm x 84cm x 75cm
Power:	Secret
Weapons:	Flip-up lid
Strengths:	Unpredictable
Weaknesses:	Unpredictable

CHAPTER 1

Hooray! Miss Boot was away on a course, which meant Mr Weakly was teaching Bertie's class this week.

"Now settle down everyone," pleaded Mr Weakly, clapping his hands.

Bertie aimed a ball of paper at Know-All Nick's head. This was going to be brilliant. Mr Weakly was as timid as a

mouse. He didn't seem to notice when
Bertie turned round or balanced a ruler
on his head. Better still, it was easy to
distract him by asking questions like, "Have
you got a girlfriend?" Mr Weakly turned as
red as a beetroot if you asked him that.

"I have some exciting news," said Mr
Weakly. "In three weeks I'm planning
to enter a team for the Junior Science
Challenge. Who wants to take part?"

Stony silence.

"This year's challenge is to build a
robot for a battle of the robots contest,"
squeaked Mr Weakly.

A robot? Bertie's hand shot up with
everyone else's. His favourite programme
on TV was *Robot Wars*, where robots
battled like gladiators. Building a robot
would be a dream come true.

"Goodness!" said Mr Weakly. "I'm afraid I can't take all of you. Write down your names and I'll try to pick a team."

After the lesson Bertie and his friends waited to add their names to the list.

"He has to choose us," said Bertie.

Darren pulled a face. "I bet he only takes teacher's pets like Know-All Nick," he said.

"I heard that!" cried Nick, turning round. "Anyway, *you* don't stand a chance, Bertie. Don't forget, you're the one who locked Mr Weakly in the store cupboard."

"Only because Darren dared me," said Bertie.

"Still, it's probably not going to help," sighed Eugene.

"Just let me talk to him," said Bertie. "We've got to be on that team."

Mr Weakly was packing away his books.

"Scuse me, sir," began Bertie. "We're dead interested in robots."

"Well, ah yes, me too," smiled Mr Weakly.

"What I mean is we'd be perfect for the team," said Bertie.

"I'm sure you would," said Mr Weakly. "But I have all the other children to consider as well."

Dirty Bertie

"I know," said Bertie. "But obviously you'll want to pick the ones who come top at science. And that's Eugene, Darren and me."

"Really?" said Mr Weakly. He couldn't picture Bertie coming top at anything.

"Imagine if we actually won the competition," Bertie went on. "Miss Boot would be dead impressed – and Miss Skinner, too!"

"Well yes, I hadn't thought of that," admitted Mr Weakly.

Dirty Bertie

It was true he wasn't Miss Skinner's favourite member of staff – mainly because his classes did what they liked.

"Well anyway, it's up to you," said Bertie. "But our names are on the list – Darren, Eugene and Bertie. I've underlined them."

Eugene closed the door behind them.

"What did you tell him that for?" he groaned. "We've never ever come top in science!"

"No, but *he* doesn't know that," grinned Bertie. "If it gets us in the team then that's all that matters."

CHAPTER 2

The next morning Mr Weakly read out
the team for the competition.

"Amanda Thribb and Nicholas," he
began.

Nick shot Bertie a look of triumph.

"And the rest of the team will be …
Darren, Eugene and Bertie," added
Mr Weakly.

Nick gasped. Bertie almost fell off his chair. They'd done it — they were in the science team!

This was going to be amazing, thought Bertie. With a little help from Mr Weakly, they were going to build the greatest robot ever!

"We don't have much time," said Mr Weakly. "So I'd like you all to design a robot for your homework. We'll let the class decide which is the best."

Dirty Bertie

For once, Bertie couldn't wait to start on his homework. He watched *Robot Wars* every week so his head was bursting with ideas. On the way home Darren and Eugene couldn't talk about anything else.

"You wait till you see my robot," said Darren. "It's going to play football."

"I'm making Spiderbot, which climbs up tall buildings," said Eugene. "What are you doing, Bertie?"

"I haven't decided yet," replied Bertie. "But it's going to be brilliant."

Back home he sat at the kitchen table with a pencil and paper. His robot had to be fast, strong and as deadly as a scorpion. It would make other robots tremble at the knees. *Let's see,* he thought. *What would be really scary?* Suddenly he had the perfect idea…

Dirty Bertie

The next day Bertie and the others handed in their homework. Mr Weakly glanced through the drawings.

"Hmm … uh huh … good grief!" he gasped when he saw Bertie's picture. "It's rather fierce!"

"That's the idea," said Bertie. "Bootosaurus will make the other robots all run away."

Dirty Bertie

"I can't say I blame them," nodded Mr Weakly.

The picture reminded him of someone but he couldn't think who it was.

"Well, let's show these to the class," he said.

Bertie stood at the front with the others and waited for his chance to explain his idea.

Dirty Bertie

"Right, let's take a vote," said Mr Weakly, handing out slips of paper. "Write down the robot you like best and I'll tot up the results."

Bertie crossed his fingers as Mr Weakly counted.

"Well, we have a winner," he said. "Darren has five votes, Eugene four, Nick … none, I'm afraid, Amanda eight and Bertie … fourteen. That means Bertie's robot is the winner."

"YESSSS!" whooped Bertie.

"NOOO!" wailed Nick.

"Oh dear!" sighed Mr Weakly.

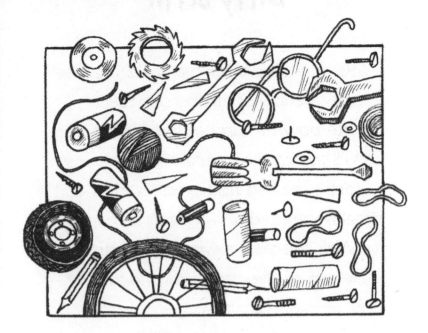

CHAPTER 3

For the next few weeks sounds of banging and hammering came from Mr Weakly's room after school. The team brought in bike lights, batteries, wheels, rubber bands and anything that might be useful. None of them had any idea how to build a robot, but luckily Mr Weakly turned out to be a whizz with a screwdriver. Finally, with a few days to go, the robot was ready.

Bootosaurus came roughly up to Bertie's waist. The body was made from a pedal bin fixed to a skateboard. It had thick glasses, pointed teeth and mad eyes. Mr Weakly said that flamethrowers were out of the question so the robot's only weapon was a flip-up lid which could catapult small objects.

Dirty Bertie

On the day of the Science Challenge, they arrived at the Pudsley Arena.

Bertie was excited to see Danny Dent from *Robot Wars* was the host.

"Woah! Check out these robots!" said Danny, looking around the hall.

"Don't worry, Bootosaurus will beat them," said Bertie.

"In your dreams," sneered Nick. "Isn't that Swotter House over there?"

Bertie recognized their old enemies who they'd beaten in the Junior Quiz.

Here they were again in their smart blazers and shiny shoes, looking for revenge.

"Don't look now, they're coming over," whispered Eugene.

Miss Topping introduced her team.

"This is Giles, Miles, Tara and Harriet," she said. "And this must be *your* robot. Goodness, what an ugly thing!"

The Swotter House team tittered and nudged each other.

"Take a look at *our* robot," boasted Giles. "We call it Shark Attack."

"It's totally invincible," bragged Tara. "That means it can't be beaten."

Bertie stared. Shark Attack was bigger than him! And it was armed with more weapons than a battleship.

"Well, good luck," said Miss Topping. "We'll be seeing you in the final round."

"The battle to the death," said Tara. "We're looking forward to that *very much*."

They marched off with their snooty noses in the air.

"Did you see their robot?" moaned Darren. "It's built like a tank!"

"Size doesn't mean anything," said Bertie. "Bootosaurus can beat them."

"Well, if we lose we'll know who to blame," said Nick.

The competition began. Danny Dent explained the first three rounds would test the robots' speed, agility and accuracy. The final round was a battle, with the last robot standing the winner.

Round one was a race round a track. Mr Weakly said they would take it in turns on the controls with Nick going first.

Shark Attack zoomed off like a streak of lightning. Bootosauraus shot backwards because Nick hit the wrong button. They trailed in second from last.

Dirty Bertie

Things didn't improve on the agility course. Amanda crashed into every obstacle and limped in fourth. Robot Golf went better although Darren and Eugene took eighteen attempts to guide a ball into a hole. Shark Attack did it in four.

After three rounds, Swotter House sat proudly at the top of the leader board. Pudsley lay back in third – second from bottom. They needed a win to stand any chance of claiming the trophy.

They broke for lunch.

"At least we're not last," said Eugene, helping himself to a slice of pizza.

"Only because Dinosnore fell over every time," said Darren.

"Shark Attack will win easily," sniffed Know-All Nick. "It's the best robot by miles. Bertie's idea was rubbish."

"It's not over yet," argued Bertie. "We've still got our secret weapon."

"Oh yes, I forgot, the flip-up lid! *Genius!*" sneered Nick.

"At least I won't steer us *backwards*," replied Bertie.

"Boys, boys, let's not argue!" sighed Mr Weakly. "We can only try our best!"

Bertie bit into his Cheesy Feast Pizza. Nick was right – Shark Attack was bigger, stronger and had better weapons. It boasted a pincer arm and a bludger blade. Bootosaurus' flip-up lid was no use at all … *or was it?*

Bertie stared at the gooey cheese pizza in his hand. It was a long shot but it might just work.

"Listen, Darren," he said. "Here's the plan…"

CHAPTER 4

A loud fanfare played as the robots entered the arena for the final round. Bertie clutched the remote controls.

Danny Dent's voice boomed over the microphone.

"So we come to the final round where our robots do battle. Remember, the last robot standing wins the round and there are double points up for grabs."

"Good luck, Bertie!" said Mr Weakly.

"Don't mess it up," hissed Nick.

Bertie watched Shark Attack spin round in circles, showing off. He'd have to keep clear of that pincer arm and bludger blade. He nodded to Darren who gave him a thumbs up.

"Robot Masters, are you ready?" asked Danny Dent. "Three, two, one… GO!"

The robots came whizzing out of their corners. Shark Attack slammed straight into Dragobot, sending it tumbling into the pit. The Swotter House team cheered wildly. Tara's eyes glinted like steel. This was going to be a breeze.

Bertie kept Bootosaurus to the edge of the arena, well out of trouble.

Dirty Bertie

"What are you playing at Bertie?" moaned Nick. "ATTACK!"

Shark Attack was back on the warpath again, eyeing its next victim. It grabbed Dinosnore in its pincer claw and tossed it aside like a used hanky.

Before long, the arena was littered with crushed and mangled robots. Dinosnore lay upside down, Dragobot was in the pit and Crackerjack was on fire. Only Bootosaurus remained to face the might of Shark Attack.

"Now we're for it," gulped Eugene.

Miss Topping leaned forwards and narrowed her eyes.

"Finish them, Tara," she ordered. "Remember the Junior Quiz."

Shark Attack closed in for the kill with its pincer arm raised. Bertie waited until he had Bootosaurus directly below them.

"NOW!" he cried.

Darren dropped something – a large slice of Cheesy Feast Pizza. It landed on top of Bootosaurus and Bertie quickly hit a button on the controls. The robot's lid flipped up, catapulting the pizza through the air.

SPLAT!

The gooey pizza landed in front of Shark Attack.

"HA! Missed!" hooted Giles.

But he spoke too soon. As Shark Attack drove over the pizza, its wheels and axles became jammed with gooey sticky cheese.

"Reverse, reverse, Tara!" screamed Miss Topping in a frenzy.

But Bertie hadn't finished. He pushed a lever. Bootosaurus shot forwards at top speed and slammed into Shark Attack. It skidded backwards towards the gaping pit. For a moment it wobbled, then it toppled in with a crash.

A huge cheer went up from the audience. Bertie breathed out.

"The winner of the final round with double points is Bootosaurus!" declared Danny Dent. "Which means Pudsley are this years' Junior Science Challenge winners!"

"We did it!" cried Eugene. "We actually won!"

"I knew we would all along," lied Know-All Nick.

Bertie looked at the Swotter House team arguing among themselves. Some people were just sore losers.

Dirty Bertie

The following Monday Bertie sat in the hall for a special assembly. Miss Skinner clasped her hands together.

"I'm very proud to tell you that Mr Weakly's team have won the Junior Science Challenge," she said. "I'd like them to come up now with their robot and Miss Boot will present the trophy."

Everyone cheered and clapped wildly. Bertie beamed – he'd never won a science trophy before.

Miss Boot shook Mr Weakly's hand.

"Well done all of you," she said. "And is this the robot you built for the competition? Does it have a name?"

Bertie gulped. His teammates stared at the floor.

Dirty Bertie

"It was actually Bertie's design," explained Mr Weakly. "He called it *Bootosaurus*."

"REALLY?" said Miss Boot coldly. "Tell me, Bertie, what gave you that idea?"